ISBN 978-1-5460-1517-8

WorthyKids
Hachette Book Group
1290 Avenue of the Americas
New York, NY 10104

Bible verse from *New Living Translation*, copyright © 1996 Tyndale House Publishers, Inc.

Library of Congress CIP data on file

Designed by Eve DeGrie

Printed and bound in China
LEO 10 9 8 7 6 5 4 3 2 1

For Keenan, Andre, Selah & Amera, who make life sweet. —B.C.

For Chrissie, Remy, and Toni. —T.B.

TASTE YOUR WORDS

Written by
BONNIE CLARK

Illustrated by
TODD BRIGHT

WORTHY®
kids

Amera's friend Maddie accidentally bumped into her at lunch.

Smash!

Amera was not happy.

"Hey! You squished my cupcake! Now I'm all sticky!" Amera snapped.

"Don't be such a crybaby," Maddie huffed.

"I'm not a crybaby, you big stink face!"

Amera took a bite of what was left of her cupcake, but it didn't taste quite the same.

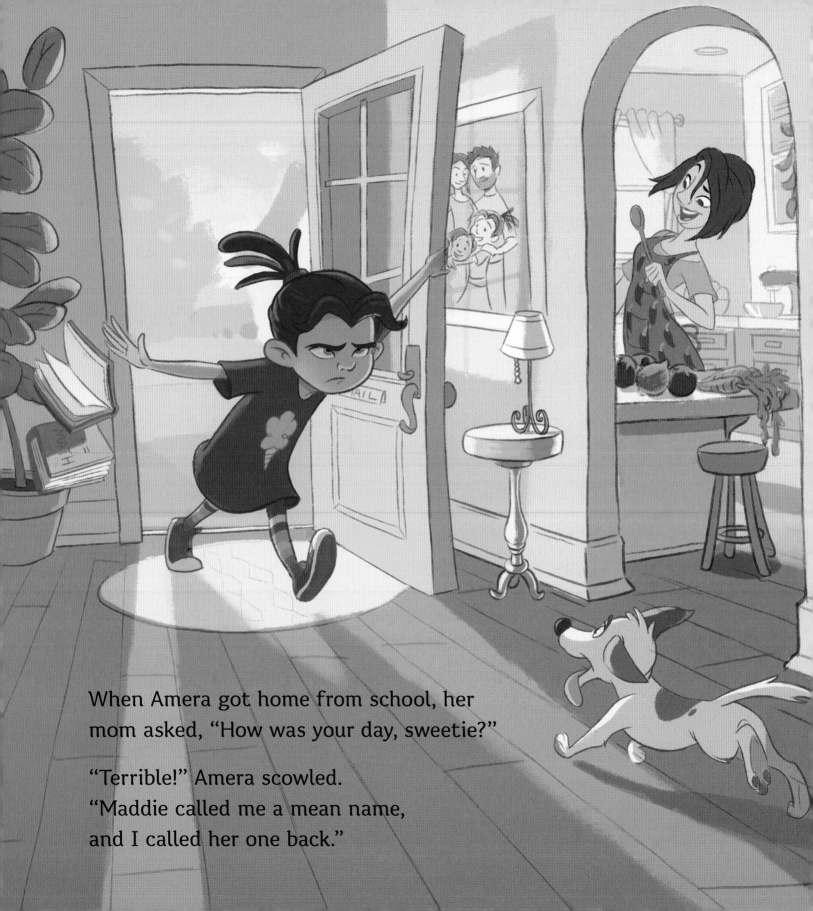

When Amera got home from school, her
mom asked, "How was your day, sweetie?"

"Terrible!" Amera scowled.
"Maddie called me a mean name,
and I called her one back."

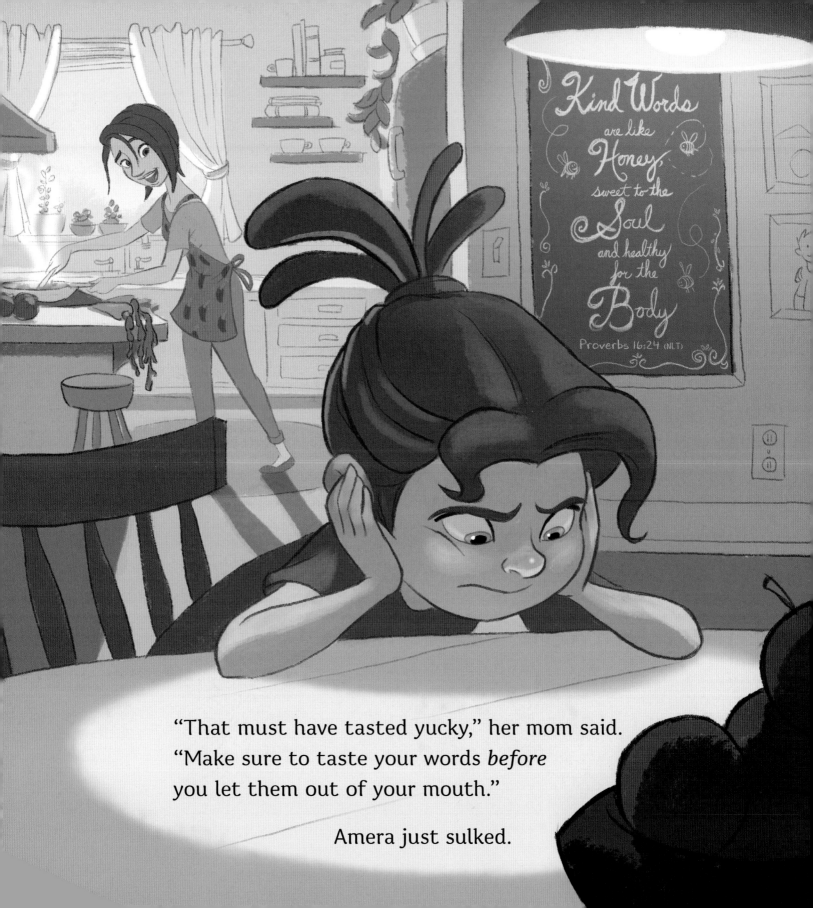

"That must have tasted yucky," her mom said. "Make sure to taste your words *before* you let them out of your mouth."

Amera just sulked.

Amera grabbed her crayons and notebook
and plopped down. Her little brother
Remy picked up a crayon.

"No! You can't color with me!
You're just a teeny-tiny baby."
When she said the words,
she tasted . . .

LEMONS AND DIRT!

"Blech!"

Amera tried to spit out the sour taste, but it lingered.

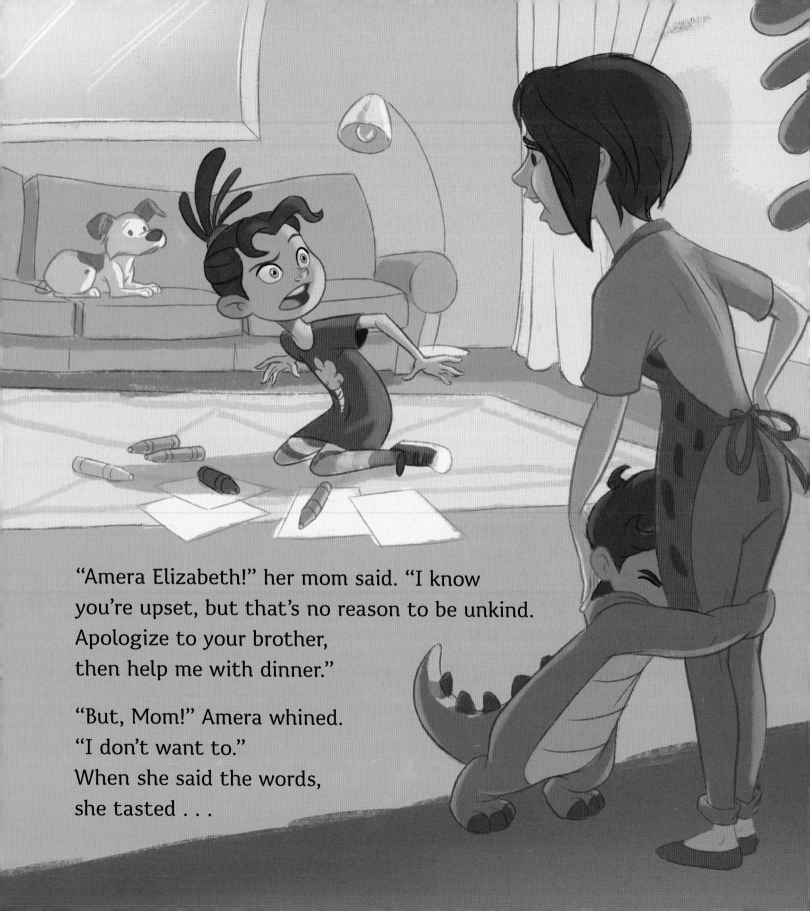

"Amera Elizabeth!" her mom said. "I know
you're upset, but that's no reason to be unkind.
Apologize to your brother,
then help me with dinner."

"But, Mom!" Amera whined.
"I don't want to."
When she said the words,
she tasted . . .

SPOILED MILK.

"Yuck!"

Amera's mom frowned.
"Go to your room!"

Amera ran up the stairs.
"This day is so stupid!"
When she said the words, she tasted . . .

ROTTEN EGGS.
"Eeew!"

Amera grabbed her toothbrush.
She scrubbed and rinsed and spit,
but the yucky taste would not leave.

She gulped large mouthfuls of water.
"I hate this!"
When she said the words,
she tasted . . .

PICKLE JUICE.
"Gah!"

Amera flopped down on her bed.

"This is ridiculous.
You can't taste words.
This is all mean Maddie's fault!"

The taste of MUD filled her mouth . . .
and tears filled her eyes.

Sitting up, Amera thought about
what her mom had told her:
  "Taste your words."

"I wonder . . . ," she said.
Amera had a delicious idea.

"I'll share!"
tasted like
BIRTHDAY CAKE.

"Can I help?"
tasted like
PEPPERMINT.

"You go first"
tasted like
ORANGES.

"Please"
tasted like
JELLYBEANS.

"That's better!"
Amera exclaimed.
She knew what
she needed to do.

Amera
dashed down
the stairs.

"Mom, I'm sorry
for all those yucky
things I said."

Cold, creamy
STRAWBERRY ICE CREAM
oozed around the two small
words. Her mom gave
Amera a squeeze.

"I'll help with dinner," said Amera.

CARAMEL!
"Yum!"

Amera ran into the next room
and scooped up her little brother.

"I'm sorry I wasn't nice to you, Remy.
Want to color with me?"

Instantly she recognized
the flavor of her favorite fruit—
WATERMELON.
Juicy and delicious.

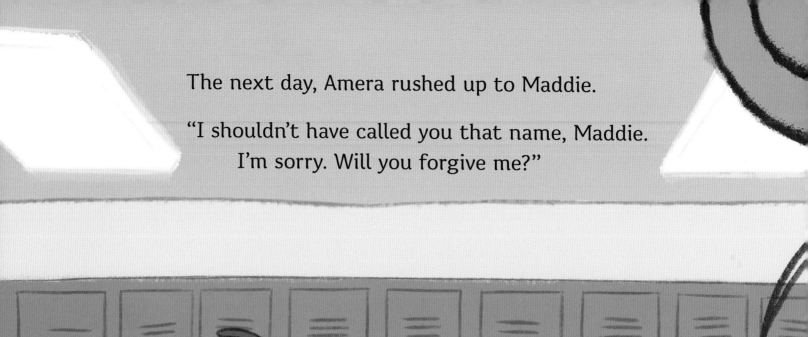

The next day, Amera rushed up to Maddie.

"I shouldn't have called you that name, Maddie.
I'm sorry. Will you forgive me?"

As soon as she apologized, Amera licked her lips.
They were sugary sweet, like

CHERRIES.

Maddie threw her
arms around Amera.
"I'm sorry too."

The day grew
sweeter as
Amera tasted
her words
in class . . .

at lunch . . .

and on the playground.

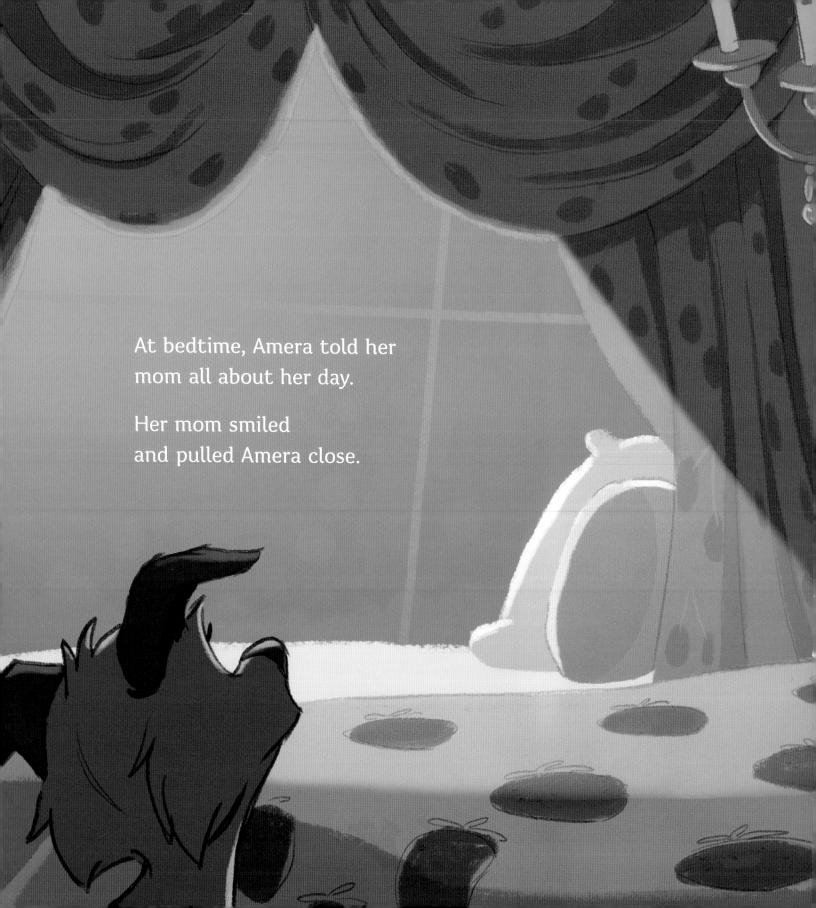

At bedtime, Amera told her
mom all about her day.

Her mom smiled
and pulled Amera close.

Just then,
    Louie leaped onto the bed
        with a shoe in his mouth.

"No, Louie!
Bad, bad dog!"
her mom said.

Louie dropped the shoe
and tucked his tail.

"Mom!" Amera said.
"Did you taste your words?"

"DOG FOOD. Yuck!"
Her mom frowned.
"I guess I need to practice
tasting my words too."

Then Amera said the yummiest words she'd tasted all day.
"I love you."

I love You

"I love you too,"
her mom said.

And they both smiled,
savoring the taste
of sweet words
drizzled in
CHOCOLATE.